"To celebrate the season and to bring joy to the long autumn nights, Queen Titania is hosting a fancy-dress party on the mainland."

"The mainland?" said Goldie. Her heart skipped a beat. She had never been to the mainland. None of the Bell sisters ever had—except Tinker Bell, of course. It was three days' flight from Sheepskerry, too long and too dangerous a journey for young fairies. Goldie kept her wings as still as she could. A fancy-dress party on the mainland? Why, she would give her *wings* to attend!

THE fairy bell SISTERS

Golden
at the
Fancy-Dress Party

Margaret McNamara

ILLUSTRATIONS BY JULIA DENOS

BALZER + BRAY
An Imprint of HarperCollinsPublishers

In the spirit of J. M. Barrie, who created Peter Pan and Tinker Bell, the author has donated a portion of the proceeds from the sale of this book to the Great Ormond Street Hospital.

Balzer + Bray is an imprint of HarperCollins Publishers.

Golden at the Fancy-Dress Party
Text copyright © 2013 by Margaret McNamara
Illustrations copyright © 2013 by Julia Denos
All rights reserved. Printed in the United States of America.
No part of this book may be used or reproduced in any manner whatsoever without written permission except in the case of brief quotations embodied in critical articles and reviews. For information address HarperCollins Children's Books, a division of HarperCollins Publishers, 195 Broadway, New York, NY 10007.
www.harpercollinschildrens.com

Library of Congress Cataloging-in-Publication Data
McNamara, Margaret.
  Golden at the Fancy-Dress Party / Margaret McNamara ; illustrations by Julia Denos. — First edition.
     pages cm. — (The fairy Bell sisters ; [#3])
  Summary: "Goldie Bell competes in Queen Titania's fancy-dress party on the mainland and needs to overcome various obstacles without the support of her sisters"— Provided by publisher.
  ISBN 978-0-06-222808-6 (hardcover bdg. : alk. paper)
  ISBN 978-0-06-222807-9 (pbk. bdg. : alk. paper)
  [1. Fairies—Fiction. 2. Costume—Fiction. 3. Contests—Fiction. 4. Sisters—Fiction.] I. Denos, Julia, illustrator. II. Title.
PZ7.M47879343Gol 2013   2013000382
[Fic]—dc23   CIP
                                                                      AC

Typography by Erin Fitzsimmons
15 16 17 CG/OPM 10 9 8 7 6 5 4 3 2
❖
First Edition

for
Isadora

THE fairy bell SISTERS

one

After all the Summer People leave Sheepskerry Island, and the goldenrod is thick on the boardwalk and the asters show their pretty purple faces, the fairies know

that fall is hastening near. The days grow shorter and the shadows longer. A chill is in the island's evening air. The sugar maples begin to hint at the blazing colors to come, the smell of wood smoke is strong, and the fairies put on gossamer shawls at night as they tell stories by the fire.

At the Fairy Bell house, Tinker Bell's little sisters—for that's who live there—were not enjoying the crisp fall day. They were arguing. That didn't happen very often, as most of the time the sisters got along splendidly. This had started as a very happy discussion, about whose job it was to stack wood in the woodpile. But then it took a wrong turn into a small misunderstanding, and from there it veered off toward ardent bickering, and now it was just short of an all-out fight.

I'm not fond of starting a story with a disagreement, so I think I'll stop for a moment to give the Fairy Bell sisters a few minutes to try to collect themselves and simmer down.

That will give us time, too, to make some introductions. If you haven't already met Tinker Bell's little sisters, their names are:

Clara Bell

Rosy Bell

Golden Bell   Sylva Bell

and baby Squeak

This story is about all the sisters, but it's mostly about Golden.

Golden Crystal Bell is a particular kind of fairy. She is a lot like her big sister Tink. She is probably the most like Tinker Bell of all the Bell sisters. Goldie is headstrong and willful, and very, very stubborn. Like Tink, she always wants to get her own way. Some people may think Goldie is a bit of a bossy-boots. But I don't think of her like that. Goldie sees the world differently than other fairies do. She notices small things that other fairies do not: the creamy shade of a hen's egg; the pattern of a spider's spots; a tiny glittering rock on the beach. She may have trouble doing certain things—I'll tell you more about that very soon—but she knows what she's good at. That's what gives Goldie her great confidence. She believes she's special. And she doesn't mind if other people believe it, too.

You may be a bit worried to read a book about such a willful, headstrong fairy.

But before you judge Goldie too harshly, let me ask you this:

Have you ever wanted to shout aloud: "I am

so much *better* than anyone else! It is so wonderful to be *me*!"

If you believe that is an improper thing to do, or even to think about doing, I'm fairly certain you will not much care for this book. Off you go.

If, however, you're even a little bit like Goldie, you might find it quite refreshing to read a book about a fairy who knows her own mind; a fairy who leaves her sisters behind to have an adventure on her own (an adventure that very nearly turns into a disaster). If that sounds like a good story to you, then please take the plunge and read on.

two

Oh, hooray! You plunged! How glad that makes me.

three

I may as well tell you what the Fairy Bell sisters were fighting about before we go much further. Fall on Sheepskerry Island is a time of bonfires and long walks in the rustling leaves. It's a time of change, and a time to prepare for winter. One of the Fairy Bell sisters' big chores is to gather firewood from the twigs and branches on the floor of the Sheepskerry forests. It's hard work, even with wings. Clara had started the woodpile back in the late spring; Rosy added to it, little by little, as the summer days went by; as fall approached, Sylva and her friend Poppy made a contest of it—who could gather the most, the quickest. (Sylva, by three twigs.) And Squeakie was too young, of course, to do more than laugh as the woodpile grew.

And Goldie? Well, so far Goldie Bell had not done too much stick gathering, it must be said. Goldie was good at avoiding work she did not like to do. What she most liked to do was to spend time experimenting with how she looked, which was what she was doing this crisp October morning.

"Honestly, Goldie, you could help with this firewood at *some* point," said Sylva from the mudroom of the Fairy Bell house. "I've done most of this week's gathering already." She stomped her feet on the doormat. "The rest is for you."

"That's nice," said Goldie absently. She was braiding her hair with ribbons she had kept from the last time Tink had sent them a package,

long ago. She loved the look of the scarlet ribbons in her hair. She imagined they might have come from Peter Pan himself. "I'll do it later."

"That's what you said last week, Golden," said Sylva. Her cheeks were red. "And you never got around to doing it."

"Well, it got done, didn't it?" asked Goldie. She was trying to concentrate on her braids. It was tricky to get them all even.

"That's because Rosy did it instead!" said Sylva.

"I can't help it if Rosy wants to do my chores," said Goldie.

"That's not the *point*!" said Sylva.

"I didn't mind doing it," said Rosy.

"You see, she didn't mind," said Goldie.

"You *always* get away with *everything*!" cried Sylva. "You can't just sit there admiring yourself. You'd better help me right now."

"I'm not just admiring myself," said Goldie.

"I'm working on these ribbons!" The scarlet ribbon was far too long. She had to concentrate to cut it in just the right place. "I'll do it, but not right *now*."

"Clara!" cried Sylva. "Make her do her chores!"

"Golden . . . ," said Clara.

"Will you *please* stop telling me what to do!" cried Goldie, and she snipped the ribbon exactly where she did not want to. "Oh no no no! That ribbon was from Tink! You made me ruin it!"

Squeak squeaked.

"*You* ruined it, not me!" cried Sylva.

Goldie's eyes filled with tears. Her lovely moment thinking about Tink and Peter Pan had been spoiled. She turned to face her sisters. "All we do on this island is work, work, work. It's not enough that we have to make our own beds and wash our own clothes and fetch the water from the pump. And go to school. And put up with all the boring Sheepskerry fairies." Even as Goldie said all this, she knew she was going too far. But once she got started, she couldn't stop. "But now it's getting to be winter, and the work will triple and it will be freezing cold and dark and *miserable*."

"Oh, Goldie," said Rosy.

Goldie brushed Rosy and her sympathy away. She threw the scarlet ribbon into the fire.

"Goldie! Don't!" cried Clara.

"Sometimes I just want to leave you all and never come back," said Goldie. Her voice was hoarse.

She flew to the mudroom and put on her boots in a fury.

"Goldie, please—"

But Goldie paid Rosy no attention.

"I hope you're happy now, Sylva," she said. Then she flew out into the cold, slamming the door behind her.

four

Things can get a bit dramatic among sisters.

By lunchtime, Goldie had come home. She had even calmed down enough to exchange two words with Sylva over lunch. "Butter?" said Goldie. "Thanks," said Sylva. By teatime, Goldie and Rosy were out in Lady's Slipper Field, watching for deer. And when the sun went down that evening, the sisters were cozy by the fireplace (made with wood gathered by Goldie), listening to Clara as she read from their favorite story.

"'Her voice was so low that at first he could not make out what she said,'" Clara read. Clara had reached one of the most exciting parts of *Peter Pan*: the moment when their big sister Tink was in the most danger. Even Squeak was perfectly quiet as Clara continued. "'Then he made it out. She was saying that she thought she could get well again if children believed in fairies.'"

They all knew what would happen next (perhaps you do too), but still it took four mugs—plus one bottle—of warm milk for them all to recover from such a dramatic moment in the story. Once they had settled down, Goldie volunteered to tuck Squeak into her crib in the great room, for it was way past her bedtime. Goldie got the blankets just right. Squeakie's tired eyes opened for a moment.

"Ma-bo-bo," said Squeak.

"I love you too, Squeakie," whispered Goldie.

Just before bed, Rosy handed Goldie her scarlet ribbons. "They're a little charred from the fire," she said. "But I know you'll find a use for them." Clara looked on and smiled.

Goldie took them from Rosy gratefully. "Sorry about all that," whispered Goldie.

"It's all right," said Clara and Rosy, at the same time.

"Time for bed," said Sylva. She gave Goldie a quick hug. Goldie hugged her back.

And the Fairy Bell sisters were at peace again.

five

The next morning was a school day. Goldie left the Fairy Bell house a little early, for today was her special time with her teacher. She was up and dressed and out of the fairy house before the sun had fully risen.

As early as it was, there was a smiling fairy teacher to greet Goldie at the door.

"Hi, Faith!" said Goldie. Faith was one of the Learned sisters, all of whom were teachers. Goldie gave Faith a hug. She loved their special time together.

"Good morning, dear Golden," said Faith.

"Come sit down and let's read together."

Now one thing you might not know about Golden Bell is that she was not much of a reader. Goldie loved stories—hearing them read aloud, and making them up herself—but she struggled with making sense of words on the page.

Sometimes words jumbled together. Sometimes they blurred. Sometimes they even jumped from one place on a page to another. Imagine how hard it was to read with the letters and words jumping all around!

That's why Goldie loved her lessons with Faith. Faith gave her all the time she needed to read and write. Like her sisters, Patience and Fortitude, Faith was a wonderful teacher.

Goldie read aloud for a bit from a book that Faith had made especially for her. (Goldie had decorated it with her own pictures.)

"'Her godmother then touched her with her wand,'" Goldie read slowly, "'and at the same instant, her clothes turned into cloth of gold and silver, all beset with jewels.'"

"Nice job, Golden!" said Faith.

"I love that story," said Goldie.

"What progress you've made!" Faith said. "You must have been working hard."

"I *have* been working hard," said Goldie. "Even if my sisters think I haven't."

"Sisters can be a trial," said Faith. "Though I do envy that you have so many of them. I'm quite lonely here at the schoolhouse, now that Patience and Fortitude have left for the Outer Islands."

Faith's two sisters had been teachers on Sheepskerry for many fairy years. But the Outer Islands needed good teachers, too, and Faith's sisters had left in the summer to teach the young fairies there.

"How I would love a little companionship, now that winter is drawing near." Faith sighed and then shook her head as if she'd been somewhere far away. "But there's no help for that. I shouldn't complain. I have all my fairy students as family." She went out to the front porch of the fairy schoolhouse and rang the bell. "And here they come now!"

With a flutter of dozens of wings, the fairies

of Sheepskerry Island flew into fairy school. All the fairies learned together and learned from one another.

Just as Faith was about to clap her hands to start their day, she was interrupted by the distant call of a conch shell.

"That's Queen Mab's clarion!" cried Faith. "It sounds as if she's on her way here! Fairies, on your best behavior, please!"

All the fairy students were amazed. Queen Mab had never come to their school before! The Fairy Bell sisters gathered together. "What can it be?" asked Sylva.

"I have no idea," said Goldie. But she noticed her wings were trembling.

Queen Mab flew to the front of the classroom. "I hope you will forgive this interruption, Faith Learned," said Queen Mab.

"Of course, my queen!" said Faith, curtsying low.

Queen Mab smiled. "My beloved fairy family," she said, her voice low. "I've had word from my dear friend on the mainland, Queen Titania."

"I hope it's not bad news," whispered Clara.

Goldie's wings quivered again. "I don't think it is," she said.

"To celebrate the season and to bring joy to the long autumn nights, Queen Titania is hosting a fancy-dress party on the mainland."

"The mainland?" said Goldie. Her heart skipped a beat. She had never been to the mainland. None of the Bell sisters ever had—except Tinker Bell, of course. It was three days' flight from Sheepskerry, too long and too dangerous a journey for young fairies. Goldie kept her wings as still as she could. A fancy-dress party on the mainland? Why, she would give her *wings* to attend!

"A fancy-dress party," whispered Poppy Flower to her best friend, Sylva. "What's that?"

"It's a dress-up party," said Sylva. "You know, with costumes!"

"Ooh!" said Poppy. "I love to dress up!"

Goldie did not say a word. She was the best at dress-up on the whole island. Everyone knew that.

"Just one fairy from each island may attend the fancy-dress party," said Queen Mab. Then she peered out and looked right at the Fairy Bell sisters. Quietly, she said to them, "Queen Titania hasn't yet learned the lesson you taught us, Sylva, at the Fairy Ball."

Sylva blushed.

Queen Mab's voice grew loud again. "There will be a prize for the best costume in Fairyland. And Queen Titania has asked us to send one fairy from Sheepskerry to take part."

"Ooh, Goldie," said Rosy. "No wonder your wings were quivering. You should go."

Goldie held her breath.

"I'd like you all to think who would create a costume that will make Sheepskerry proud," said Queen Mab. "I would rather show pride in our fairy island than win, as I'm sure you know."

Queen Mab paused for a bit, to let the fairies talk among themselves. The Cobweb sisters knit the best shawls and sweaters, but the Stitch sisters were the best at sewing and dressmaking.

"The Stitch sisters can sew anything," said Acorn Oak. "I think one of them should go."

The three Stitch sisters—Fern, Satin, and Daisy—put their heads together.

"They sew so beautifully," said Poppy. "In a way it's right that one of them should go."

"But in a way it's not," said Clara. "We all know that Goldie would be the best at making a costume. But we must let the fairies decide. That's the Fairy Way."

Fern Stitch flew straight up to Queen Mab. The Fairy Bell sisters could not hear what she was saying, but later they heard about the conversation from Iris Flower, who heard it from Sugar Bakewell. "It's true we are known far and wide for our tiny stitching and intricate patterns," Fern had told the queen. "But all three of us think someone else should go to the mainland. Someone else who will make the best costume in the land."

As soon as Fern stepped away from Queen Mab, there was a murmuring in the crowd, as if all the fairies were speaking with one voice. At first it sounded like they were saying, "*Go! Go!*" But then Clara and Rosy and Sylva—and, of course, Goldie—heard more clearly what their fairy friends were saying.

"*Gold-ie! Gold-ie!*" came the cheer.

"Listen!" said Clara.

"I'm listening!" cried Goldie.

"GOLD-IE! GOLD-IE! GOLD-IE!"

"Golden Bell, please come up before me," said Queen Mab.

Goldie flew over in a rush. Her wings had stopped trembling now.

On her way she turned to the Stitch sisters. "Oh, Fern, are you very sure?" asked Goldie. "Would you really give up your place for me?"

"Of course I would," said Fern Stitch. "I don't really want to go to the mainland. Not that much, anyway."

"Besides, it's awfully hard work making a costume," said Daisy.

"Oh, thank you!" said Goldie, giving them a huge smile. Then she curtsied to Queen Mab, just as her teacher had. "And I most humbly thank you, Queen Mab," she said.

"Don't thank me," said Queen Mab. "Thank your fairy friends."

Goldie looked out at the happy faces of her

sisters and her schoolmates.

"Oh, I will make you proud, Sheepskerry fairies!" she cried. "I will make Sheepskerry Island very proud indeed!"

six

The next day was misty and gray, but Goldie's mood was the complete opposite. She dressed before dawn in a traveling outfit: a royal-blue suit with pink polka-dot piping. And matching polka-dot shoes.

Goldie had hardly slept a

wink all night. Queen Mab had given her instructions about what to do on the mainland, and her head was swimming. Goldie would stay in a big house with the other fairies who were going to the fancy-dress party. *We'll be best friends!* Goldie thought. She'd be allowed to choose seven items from Queen Titania's Magical Costume Trunk, and from those she would put together her costume. And the costume was to be based on a theme chosen by the queen. *Please let Queen Titania choose a good theme for the costumes!* Goldie thought. *I don't want to dress as a piece of fruit!* That idea alone kept her up for an hour. Then she spent a long time picturing herself on a mainland boulevard, lightly flying next to two or three mainland fairies who had become her fast friends. She imagined the cheers as she entered the fancy-dress party in her gorgeous attire.

Goldie regarded her sweet little suit in her full-length mirror. She tied a navy-blue ribbon in her hair. *Nice!* she thought. Unfortunately, the ferry ride would be cold and wet, so she'd also have to wear a hefty oilskin coat to keep warm and dry.

"My yellow coat?" Goldie asked her reflection in the mirror. "Or the green one?"

Clara called from downstairs. "Goldie! The tide is turning! You'll miss the ferry!"

"Coming, Clara!" said Goldie. "Green, I think. To show off my hair. I just wish it wouldn't frizz so in this weather!" She leaned down to pick up her luggage—three carpetbags full to bursting. (One was only for shoes.) She could barely carry them all.

"Sylva! Rosy! Can you help me with my bags?"

Rosy flew up the stairs. "Oh my goodness, Goldie!" she said. "Do you really need to take that much? It's just for the weekend."

"I'm sure most fairies could get along without

very many clothing choices," said Goldie. "But I cannot. Not to mention shoes. Oh, where are those little dancing slippers I like so much? Can I fit them in?"

"There won't be dancing at the party, I don't think," said Rosy. "So you could leave your slippers at home. And isn't that *my* green coat?"

"I thought you'd want me to have it for the weekend, Rosy. It looks so good on me on a rainy day like this."

Goldie hoped Rosy would say yes, and she did, with her smile.

"Come on, Golden," said Sylva. "The ferry won't wait."

And in a moment the bags were gathered, and all five Fairy Bell sisters were out the door. They flew down the boardwalk to the dock, Goldie collecting cobwebs and shells from the path and stuffing them in her pockets. "I may need these for my costume," she said. Clara carried Squeak in her arms as she hurried Goldie along. Just before they got to the dock, Squeak looked at Goldie with her big brown eyes. "Doh-ca!" she said.

"There, there, little Squeak," said Goldie. "I can't possibly take you to the mainland. You'll go when you're a grown-up fairy, like I am."

"Don't you wish, just a little bit, that we were all going together?" asked Sylva. "I don't much care about the mainland, but we're always—"

"I know. We are *always* together," said Goldie. "But I can't just be on this tiny little island all my life. I need to get out and spread my wings."

"Of course you do, Goldie," said Clara. "We all want to grow up." Goldie thought she noticed a catch in Clara's voice. "This is your turn to shine."

They heard a splashing in the water.

"There's Merryweather!" cried Sylva.

Merryweather was an unusual ferry. She

wasn't a boat at all; she was a gray seal who stopped by Sheepskerry once a month to take fairies on the long trip to the mainland. I don't know if you've ever seen seals swimming, but they look rather like dogs when they're paddling. They can swim for a long time with their sleek heads above the water and their noses pointed exactly where they want to go.

Merryweather gave three hoarse barks.

"That's the signal," said Clara. "Time for you to get on, Golden."

Goldie turned to say her good-byes. "Bye-bye, little Squeakie," she said. She held Squeak close. "I wonder how much you'll change while I'm gone."

"Good-bye, Goldie!" cried Rosy. "I know you'll do beautifully. Take good care of yourself! And say hello to Lulu if you see her on the mainland!"

"I will!" said Goldie. Lulu was Rosy's

friend—a human child. Human people made
Goldie a little nervous, but how lovely it would
be to see Lulu again!

"We'll be here on the dock waiting when you
come back," said Clara.

Goldie flew over to Merryweather's jet-
black head and settled comfortably in the seal's
sleek fur. Her luggage just fit, even if it might get

a little wet. Merryweather gave one more bark and paddled away.

And as if they had planned it, Clara, Rosy, and Sylva took a silent breath together and sang in harmony:

The water is wide;
You will soon pass o'er.
And then you'll find
A land a-new.
Sheepskerry's strength
Will give you hope,
Till you return,
Our sister true.

Goldie looked out to the distant horizon. Then she turned and waved once more to her sisters on the dock. "At last," Goldie said to herself. "I'm Golden Crystal Bell. And I'm on my own."

seven

"There she is! There she is!" Goldie heard the calls even before Merryweather was at the mainland ferry station.

Three very beautiful and very elegantly dressed fairies were waving a greeting. Goldie started to wave back—but then she realized they weren't waving at her. She lowered her hand.

"I don't mind," said Goldie to Merryweather. "I'm going to do fine here."

But as Goldie looked around at the unfamiliar setting, her courage failed her for a moment.

The mainland was a lot different from Sheep-skerry.

There were no human people in sight, which was a relief, but Golden had never seen so many fairies. Not at the Fairy Ball; not at Queen Mab's island meetings; not even in her dreams. How could there be so many fairies in one place? She gave Merryweather a quick kiss (that was her payment!) and unsteadily flew down the gang-plank to the fairy town.

Goldie saw fairies of every age and shape and size. They were all in a terrible hurry. And if they noticed Golden Bell at all, it was only to tell her to get out of the way.

But oh, what an extraordinary place this was!

Buildings crowded the streets—not just fairy houses for one family, but gigantic fairy houses that must have fit a dozen or a score or a hundred fairies all together. The fairy houses were so high they seemed to reach almost to the sky. Instead of trees and flowers, there were long roads and pigeon buses. And looming up above the town were two enormous buildings. Goldie could read their big signs—one was the Museum of Fairy History; the other, the Gallery of Fairy Art.

Goldie was dazzled.

"Don't stand there gawking," said an elderly fairy to Goldie. "Or if you do, at least move out of the way, so an old fairy like me can get by."

"Oh, of course," said Golden. "May I ask, do you know the way to—"

But before Goldie could finish her question, the elderly fairy had flown away.

How does anyone find her way here? Goldie thought. But then she remembered the instructions Queen Mab had given her. A fairy named Avery would greet her at the ferry dock, and then take her to stay with two mainland fairies,

Claudine and Amanda Townley. *One thing at a time,* Goldie thought.

"Avery, Avery. Where is she?" said Goldie. She half wished she could squeeze Rosy's hand right now, or that Clara would take charge. She was even feeling that sometimes she was a little too harsh with Sylva—

"Golden? Golden Bell of Sheepskerry?"

"Yes, that's me."

"I'm Avery Pastel, Claudine and Amanda's serving fairy." Avery was neat and pretty, and she smiled at Golden shyly. "Welcome to the mainland."

"I'm very pleased to meet you, Avery," said Golden.

"Let me take those," said Avery. She picked up two of Golden's bags.

"Oh, thank you so much," said Golden. "They're very heavy."

Avery looked startled. "You don't have to

thank me," she said. "I'm a serving fairy." She led Goldie to an elegant carriage. "You sit here," she said, settling Goldie into a comfortable seat. Then Avery took a seat on a bench at the back of the carriage. "To the town house!" she said to the carriage driver, a bright-eyed sparrow. And off they flew.

As the two fairies made their way over the tall buildings in the afternoon sun, Goldie and Avery chatted about the mainland and what life was like there. "We don't have serving fairies on Sheepskerry," Goldie said.

Avery was so startled she almost bounced

right off her bench. "No serving fairies?" she said. "How do you manage?"

"We do a lot of things for ourselves," said Golden. "The cooking and cleaning, the laundry, the baby-fairy minding. Even the wood chopping, though I'm not much good at that."

"The serving fairies take care of that kind of thing here. Fairies like you—they don't have to lift a wing."

"Oh, how marvelous!" sang Goldie. If she had been paying attention, she might have seen that Avery's face fell a little. "I could get used to this!"

eight

When Avery and Golden arrived at the Townley sisters' house, Goldie was exhausted from her journey, but not exhausted enough to miss out on any detail. "A crystal chandelier!" she cried. "And look at this staircase! It curves!" Golden imagined herself floating slowly down the staircase with her fancy-dress costume on. She imagined the other fairies looking at her with wonder and disbelief. Could a Sheepskerry fairy really be so stylish? "You bet!" said Goldie.

"I'm sorry?" A cool voice interrupted

Goldie's dream.

Goldie spun around to find two very pretty and very fashionable fairies staring at her. "Oh, no, I'm sorry!" Goldie said. "I was thinking out loud!" Her face turned pink. "I'm Golden Bell, from—"

"Oh yes, we know where you're from," said one of the fairies. "You're from"—and she paused; Goldie thought she heard a little sniff—"Sheepskerry Island. I suppose you're a shepherdess?"

The other pretty fairy giggled.

"No, there aren't sheep there anymore," said Goldie. She thought the fairies were teasing her, but she couldn't tell.

"Um . . . are you Amanda and Claudine?" Goldie asked.

The two fairies looked down their pert little noses. "Who else would we be?" said the taller one. "I'm Claudine. I and Amanda own

this house. Queen Titania has made us host all
twelve fairies for the fancy-dress party. From the
mainland *and* the islands."

"Avery, take her coat, please," said Claudine.
"How quaint it is, too," she added quietly, but
not so quietly that Goldie did not hear. Goldie
was glad she had worn her little blue suit as her

arrival outfit. *They can't make fun of this*, she thought.

"It's very kind of you to have invited us all to stay with you," said Goldie, using her best manners, even though the Townley sisters were being not so polite themselves. "I adore your house," she said. "It is so elegant! And so huge! You must love living here."

"*Humph!*" said Amanda. "I suppose you haven't seen many *real* fairy houses before."

"I've seen almost all the houses on Sheepskerry, plus the summer cottages," said Goldie. "So I think I do know pretty well what a fairy house looks like."

Amanda and Claudine smiled. "Not a *mainland* fairy house," said Amanda.

Then they turned to go. "We will see you at supper," said Claudine. "That will give you time to change"—she paused, and arched an eyebrow—"into something suitable."

Goldie felt her cheeks turn pink.

"Move these bags, will you?"

Goldie reached for her carpetbags. "I'm sorry. Are they in your—"

"Please, Golden. Avery carries bags here," said Amanda.

"I'll just take these upstairs," said Avery to Goldie. Then she whispered, "Never mind them. Not all mainland fairies are so snobby. Come on up with me. I'll get you settled in."

nine

The sting of Claudine and Amanda's unfriendly greeting felt less keen as Goldie looked in wonder at the bedroom where she was to stay. Instead of curtains made of oak leaves, there were delicate water-silk panels of shell pink. A sweet gold-and-white vanity—with a three-way mirror!—was nestled in a corner. A plush rose carpet was on the floor. And the bed! Goldie flew over and fell onto the pillowy down comforter. "There's nothing like this on Sheepskerry!" she said.

"It's nice, isn't it?" said Avery without even

looking around. "I'll leave you now so you can have a moment's peace before supper."

"That sounds good," said Goldie. "Will you sit next to me at the dinner table, Avery? I have to admit I'm a little nervous around those Townley sisters."

Avery shook her head. "Oh, no!" she said. "I never sit at the table, especially not on a grand occasion like this! Why, there must be a dozen fairies staying here at least! I'll eat with Caraway Cooke in the kitchen, after you've had your meal."

Goldie's face fell. The mainland kept surprising her.

"Will there be anything else, miss?" asked Avery.

"Please, call me Goldie!"

Avery smiled a cautious smile. "Will there be anything else, Goldie?" she asked.

"There is one thing." Goldie wanted to

ask why the Townley sisters seemed so . . . unfriendly. But she didn't want Avery to think she couldn't handle herself on the mainland.

"If you're wondering why Amanda and Claudine are so unfriendly," said Avery, "the reason is that the Townley sisters win the fancy-dress prize every single year. All the mainland fairies seem to think that's the way it *has* to be." Avery busied herself by unpacking Goldie's bags. "But now the island fairies have been invited, and Amanda and Claudine have heard that island fairies are very good at creating things out of bits and pieces. Especially you."

"Oh my!" said Goldie.

"And that's why they are *not* on their best behavior." The little porcelain clock on the mantelpiece struck five. "Now I must fly," said Avery. She slipped out the door, and Golden was on her own.

"I'd better change into a different dress,"

said Goldie to herself. "Which means I'll have to redo my nails, too. I hope I'll be fancy enough for dinner!"

As she got ready, Goldie thought a lot about what Avery had told her. *How nice that people are saying I'm good at creating things!* she thought. *But how sorry I am that Claudine and Amanda are cross about it.*

When she was dressed and her nails were drying, Goldie flew over to the window to get a breath of fresh fall air. She looked out on the cityscape below her. "What a lot of lights!" she said. Goldie gazed up at the stars, but she couldn't make them

out for the bright city glow. Then she strained her eyes toward the harbor to see if she could glimpse the ocean, or the islands beyond. She could not. "Oh well," said Goldie, with a small sigh. "I know they're home and safe on Sheep-skerry."

I'm sure you can guess who was on Goldie's mind!

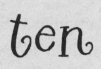

ten

Dinner that night was not so bad. The food was delicious, and the conversation was lively. All the other fairies—even the ones from the mainland— were perfectly nice. Fawn Deere, from Doe Isle, seemed almost like a friend. Avery was so busy serving that Golden hardly caught a glimpse of her, but when she did, they exchanged smiles. If Claudine and Amanda hadn't made their guests feel so nervous, Goldie and the visiting fairies might have had a lovely time.

After dinner, when she went up to her

bedroom, Goldie was so exhausted from her long day that she fell asleep the moment she sank down into her pillows. She didn't hear the din of carriages and the murmur of voices and the whir of fairy wings passing her windows all night long. She slept soundly, and dreamt of seals, spruce trees, and a carpetbag with wings.

In the morning she woke early. On Sheepskerry she always rose with the sun, and she could not change her habits in one day. Not to mention that the fancy-dress party was this very evening! How could anyone sleep!

Goldie dressed quickly—for her—in a floaty little high-waisted dress with a lovely print of crimson poppies. And red boots. She swept her hair into a high ponytail, hastily made up her bed, and decided to go downstairs to explore. "I'll fix myself some breakfast before they wake up," she said to herself.

The big, long hallway was silent and still. Goldie crept past the closed doors of bedroom after bedroom and found her way down the stairs. The Townley dining room was empty. Nor was there anyone in the parlor, though a fire was burning brightly. "Aha!" said Goldie to herself. "Someone's been up and about."

She hadn't noticed it last night at supper, but there was a little doorway off to the side of the dining room. She opened it carefully. It led to a wide stairway, and Goldie heard the clatter of the kitchen at the base of it. *So that's where the food comes from*, she said to herself. *I thought it was magic!*

The kitchen was a hive of activity. There was a fairy cook with an open, cheerful face. *She must be Caraway*, thought Goldie. Next to her flitted another fairy, but she was working so quickly Goldie could hardly tell who it was.

Then she realized—

"Avery!" she said.

"Oh my goodness, miss! What are you doing here? All the fairies are asleep."

"No, they're not," said Goldie. "You're a fairy, and you're up and working away. What can I do to help?"

"I'm Caraway Cooke," said the older fairy. "And since you're here, keep yourself out of the way. You modern fairies don't know how to do much of anything, anyway. Not like my dear sister, Saffron, though of course there's no room for her in *this* house." Avery waggled her eyebrows at Golden at that remark. "Avery, tend that fire. It's not hot enough for me to put the scones in."

"But I'm squeezing the oranges—"

"Then hurry up about it, please." Caraway Cooke was not unkind, but she was very, very firm. She pointed to a small sheet of paper

pinned up on the wall. "Try again to read the note I left you."

Goldie looked over to where Caraway Cooke was pointing. There was a long list pinned to a corkboard. There were funny little doodles drawn all over it.

Avery flew over to consult the list of jobs for the day. She stared at it for a long time.

Goldie flew over to her side.

"I like the drawings," said Goldie. "Did you do those?"

Chores

AVERY   CARAWAY

DUST

SWEEP   MENUS

TEND   COOKING
FIRE   PANTRY

PEEL   SHOPPING
POTATOES   BAKING

WASH DISHES

MOP

Avery nodded. "I like to draw," she said. She was staring at the list. "Could you just . . . read it to me?"

Goldie could tell it was hard for her to ask. She smiled. "I'm not very good at reading," she said.

Caraway Cooke dropped a spoon. Avery's wings nearly stopped.

"Not very good at reading?" said Avery.

"Then why aren't you a—"

"Who's not very good at reading?" Claudine's voice cut through the kitchen. She was floating at the top of the stairs.

"I'm—" Goldie began.

"Um, what she *means*," Avery said quickly, "is she's not going to make a big fuss about *my* reading trouble. Breakfast will be along in just a few more minutes."

"See that it is," said Claudine. "Golden, you should be upstairs. This way, please."

"I'm coming," said Goldie, but she stayed right where she was. Claudine did not look happy.

"What was all that about?" asked Golden when Claudine had shut the door. "Why can't I say that I'm—"

"Don't you know?" asked Avery.

"Know what?" asked Golden.

"Don't you know," said Caraway Cooke very

quietly, "that fairies who aren't good at reading or numbers become serving fairies here on the mainland?" She put the scones in the oven and closed the door fiercely. "I'm a cook because I'm a Cooke sister, and it's what I love to do. I'd very much like to have my younger sister working here too, but the Townley fairies prefer Avery—she comes cheap."

Caraway wiped her hands on her apron. "Avery's drawings should be in the Gallery of Fairy Art, but she has such trouble reading, don't you, Avery?" Caraway looked at her with great tenderness. "I do my best here, but I'm no teacher. And she has no sisters to help her. She has no one at all."

eleven

Before we go any further, I think I'd better tell you how it is that Avery had no fairy sisters, and Goldie had so many. It's no secret that a fairy is born when a human child laughs for the first time. The Fairy Bell sisters were born of a particularly happy child; Becca was her name, and she had a bright, musical laugh. Baby Becca laughed for the first time one morning in the sunroom of her family's house as her parents cooed over her. "*Ha-hah! Hah! Aaah! Laha-ha-ha! Ho-ho!*" There was a pause . . . and then she giggled a last "*Hee-hee!*" and finally she took a breath. (It was a big laugh for a first timer.)

Becca's "*Ha-hah!*" became Tink; the second "*Hah!*" was Clara. "*Aaah!*" was Rosy, "*Laha-ha-ha!*" was Golden, "*Ho-ho!*" was Sylva, and that last "*Hee-hee!*" was, of course, baby Squeak.

The Fairy Bell sisters had a happy birth indeed!

But some fairies have a different beginning. Occasionally, a very sullen child manages a first laugh late in life. "*Humph! Hamph!*" Usually such a child is not laughing in delight, but laughing at another's misfortune. From that sort of laugh, very unpleasant fairies are born. (Claudine and Amanda were surely the products of a "*Humph! Hamph!*")

Avery was born of a very happy human child called Emma, who managed to laugh earlier than all the other babies but didn't quite recognize what she was doing. Some infants are that way—they laugh before they know what they're about, and it scares them quite out of their little baby wits. Emma's first laugh came when she was fingerpainting (with applesauce). It was part "*Hah!*" and part "*Hic!*" She was so scared of her own laugh that she didn't giggle again till she was walking. (Ask your parents sometime what your first laugh sounded like. If you were a "*Hah!/Hic!*" perhaps your laugh gave birth to a fairy like Avery.)

"Avery's teachers gave up on her," said Caraway Cooke in the silent kitchen, "and sent her here to work in the kitchen when she was just a mite. A serving fairy is what she'll be all her life. For the likes of Claudine and Amanda." Caraway sniffed.

"They gave up on you?" Golden couldn't imagine such a thing. She thought of Faith and her fairy school. Faith would never give up on any of her students! Especially not Goldie! "That's terrible!" she said.

"Isn't that how it is on Sheepskerry?"

"No!" said Goldie. "On Sheepskerry, the teachers know that every fairy is good at different things. Not every fairy learns the same way."

"You'd better not let the mainland fairies hear you talk that way," said Avery.

"And you'd best get upstairs for breakfast," said Caraway. "The other fairies will be wondering what you're doing talking to Avery. Get on with you, now. And don't come back."

twelve

Goldie could barely concentrate as she went upstairs to breakfast. The other fairies were talking in high-pitched, excited voices and flitting about the breakfast table. They were chattering so loudly that they didn't notice how quiet Goldie was.

The single topic of conversation was what this year's fancy-dress theme would be.

"I bet it will be Famous Fairies from History," said Fawn. "If it is, I'll go as Tinker Bell!"

Goldie knew she should say something about her famous sister, but she was too lost in thought to say a word.

"I hope it's Magic Animals," said a fairy named Arabella. She was a mainland fairy, and seemed much kinder than the Townley sisters. "I would be a magical unicorn."

The other fairies chimed in.

"And I'd be a dragon!"

"And I'd be a phoenix with rainbow wings!"

"It's no use guessing," said Claudine. "We won't know what the theme is until Queen Titania's decree arrives."

Goldie's mind was still on Avery. "The unfairness of it all!" she said aloud.

The fairies were silent.

"Golden Bell?" said Amanda. "Are you saying our queen is unfair?"

"Your queen?" said Goldie. She was embarrassed that she had not been following the conversation.

"Queen Titania sends us a decree on the

morning of the party. The decree contains the costume theme." Amanda spoke to Goldie as if she were a simpleton. "Then we observe a code of fairy silence till all the costumes are made."

"That's the way it has always been done," said Claudine. "And the way we'll do it this year—even with you island fairies here. There's nothing unfair about it."

"Oh, I didn't mean—"

There was a sharp rap at the front door.

"Queen Titania's page!"

A young fairy in smart gold brocade arrived on the doorstep of Amanda and Claudine's house. She presented Amanda with a scroll.

All the fairies gathered around the decree with great excitement.

"Remember! Silence from now on," said Amanda. She unrolled the scroll and hung it up on the wall behind her.

Goldie just hoped that the costume theme

would be something perfect for her. *But whatever it is,* she thought, *I'll do my best for Sheepskerry.*

When she looked at the scroll, her face fell. It was in very fancy handwriting. It must have been written by Queen Titania herself!

All the fairies gathered around Queen Titania's decree. None of them made a sound. Golden looked up at the wall of words and did what Faith told her to do. She took a deep breath and focused her eyes on the swirling words, one at a time. But still the letters pushed together, and the words floated around the page. She could only make out a word here and there.

Dress   fairy

nature   MAGICAL

help

Where was Clara, who read to her every night? Or Rosy, who would have whispered every word written on the scroll? Where was Sylva, who'd say the code of silence was silly and everyone should help one another?

Goldie's wings were shaking, and she was sure her face was pale as birch bark. What if she did not know what kind of costume she was to wear to the party?

The fairies began to float away, one by one, all with great grins on their faces. Soon only Claudine was left. Golden took a break from trying to read the scroll. She looked over at Claudine for a moment.

"Whatever's the matter, Golden Bell?" Claudine whispered.

Goldie shook her head. She did not want to break the code of silence!

"Queen Titania won't mind if we talk a little now," said Claudine. "The competition doesn't start officially till the Magical Treasure Chest arrives."

"Truly?" asked Golden.

"Truly," said Claudine. "Honest."

"It's just that—"

"You have trouble reading, don't you, Golden?" said Claudine.

It was the first time it felt hard to reply to that question. "Yes," she said. "I do."

If Goldie had not been looking down at her sweet little red boots, she might have seen a very small smile cross Claudine's face. "Not to worry," Claudine told Golden. "Here. Let me read it to you."

Claudine turned to face the scroll on the wall. This is what she told Goldie it said:

"Titania, queen of the mainland, does hereby announce and decree that each fairy attending the FANCY-DRESS

PARTY shall create her own costume (in silence, with no help from others), using seven items from QUEEN TITANIA'S MAGICAL COSTUME TRUNK and elements from nature. Each fairy shall dress in the manner of a W I T C H."

Claudine paused. "Got that, Goldie?" she asked.

"Got it," said Goldie. "Thank you, Claudine! Thank you so much. I'll make the best witch costume ever."

Claudine smiled. "You do that, Golden Bell," she said. "And may the best fairy win."

thirteen

P recisely one hour later, Queen Titania's Magical Costume Trunk appeared in the Townley sisters' parlor in a puff of sparkling smoke, and all the fairies gathered around to wait for it to open.

"One at a time!" called Amanda. "I'm first. The rest of you get behind me."

Goldie was dying to push her way to the front so she could have her pick of the items in the trunk for her witch costume. But she waited with the others behind Amanda and Claudine.

"You were last to breakfast this morning,

Golden," said Amanda. "So all of us think you should be last in line, don't we, fairies?"

The other fairies said nothing.

"I suppose that's fair," said Goldie, though she wasn't convinced.

The magical trunk opened with a peal of fairy bells. Goldie waited and waited as all the other fairies floated up to the trunk and flew away with their choices. *I hope there are a few good things left for me!* she thought. Finally Fawn Deere flew out with a wink to Goldie. She had chosen an armful of pink and sparkly items, which Goldie thought was rather odd, considering the witchy theme. But she didn't have time to think about it. It was her turn to choose.

The magical trunk was a massive old leather box, but it crackled and sparkled, and it was packed with bits and pieces that would be perfect for costume making. Even after a dozen other fairies had taken their share of pieces, it was still full to the brim.

A treasure trove of jewels and shiny skirts and a pair of white opera gloves lay on top of the pile. Goldie looked at them longingly, and since she couldn't resist, she tried them on.

"How beautiful I would look if I went to the party in these lovely things!" she sighed as she gazed in a little mirror. "But they're not for this witch!"

Just underneath a pair of pink stockings, Goldie was a little surprised to find a bolt of black taffeta and a length of deep purple lace. And under that, she spotted a shiny pointed hat and an old crooked broom.

"Perfect!" she said. "I can't believe the other fairies left these for me!" She put her four choices aside. Now she had three more.

She chose some scuffed black slippers and a length of shimmering silk chiffon. Then she spotted a makeup kit. "Whoa-ho!" she said. "I can give myself green skin with this! And a warty nose!"

Goldie considered herself in the mirror that hung over the parlor fireplace. She peered in close and turned her head so she could see her charming profile. "I imagine the other fair-ies don't dare look too witchy," she said, "but I'm not afraid. I want to be the best witch the mainland has ever seen, and if it means I grow a warty nose, then a warty nose it will be!"

fourteen

All that afternoon, Goldie worked on her costume. She trimmed the pointy hat with sea urchins she had brought from Sheepskerry's west shore. She snipped and stitched and made the bolt of black taffeta into a swirling cape lined with purple lace, and sewed deep blue mussel shells on the collar. "Reversible!" Goldie exclaimed with delight as she tried it on.

Her gown was made of sheer black chiffon, with a long white lining (her nightgown!) underneath it. Goldie had made pointy shoes out of the pair of old slippers she'd found at the bottom of the costume box, and she painted her best white stockings with red stripes.

Goldie's costume was almost done when there was a knock at the door. Avery peeked her head inside.

"Can I come in?" she asked. Then she started in surprise. "Oh! I'm sorry. I thought this was Golden's room!"

Goldie burst into laughter.

"Oh, it is you!" cried Avery. "I didn't even recognize you when I came in. You look *horrible!*"

Goldie didn't want to break the code of

silence, but she gave Avery a gap-toothed grin.

"You can talk to me, Goldie. I'm not in the contest!"

"Whew!" said Golden. "It's so good to talk at last! I'm just going to put some cobwebs on my wings and then I'll be done," she said. "Lucky thing I brought those cobwebs from Sheepskerry!" She had to twist sideways to get the right effect. "Don't help me! I don't want to cheat!" She draped some stringy webs on her wingtips. "How are the other fairies doing?" she asked, hoping they were not quite as witchy as she was.

"I haven't seen anyone else," said Avery. "All their doors are closed. And I only wanted to see *you!*"

Goldie glued one more wart on her nose. "Time to go!" she said. "How do I look?"

"You are the scariest witch I have ever seen!"

Goldie spun around and looked at herself in the mirror, every way she could.

"If I'm not the ugliest witch at this fancy-dress party," she said, "I'll eat my pointy hat!"

fifteen

The clock on the mantel chimed six times.

Goldie opened the door to her room and peered out into the hallway. "I wonder where all the other fairies are," she said. "I'm not late, am I?"

"No," said Avery. "You're right on time."

"They must already have gathered in the entrance hall. Come on, let's hurry!"

Goldie and Avery flew to the top of the winding staircase. At last they heard fairy chatter coming from downstairs. "I'm coming!" cried Goldie. "Hold on!"

When Goldie spoke, the fairy chatter died down. Goldie didn't notice the quiet, though; she was so excited to make her entrance. She closed her eyes at the top of the staircase. It was all just as she had dreamed it would be. "Here I am!" she called. "I fly for Sheepskerry and Queen Mab!"

There was a moment of absolute silence. Goldie's eyes popped open. And then . . . there was an enormous gale of laughter.

"She's a witch!"

"She's hideous!"

"Didn't she read the decree?"

"Look! She's got warts on her nose!"

If Goldie's face had not been green, the other fairies would have seen her cheeks turn scarlet from humiliation and shame. If the brim of

her hat had not hidden her eyes, the other fairies would have seen tears welling up in them. And if any of the other fairies had noticed the broom she was sitting on, they would have seen it shaking.

"Oh, Goldie! Fly away!" cried Avery behind her. "Don't you see? They tricked you!"

Shall I tell you now what Queen Titania's invitation really said? Or have you already guessed? If you have, your heart will have gone out to dear, trusting Goldie.

Here's the invitation, and it *is* quite tricky to read. You can read it yourself, or you can ask someone to read it for you, if you'd prefer. I do so hope that where you're reading this it's not like the fairy mainland. I do so hope that you have a friend or a sister or a teacher like Faith!

Titania,
queen of the mainland,
does hereby announce and decree
that each fairy attending the
FANCY-DRESS PARTY
shall create her own costume
(in silence, with no help from others),
using seven items from
QUEEN TITANIA'S
MAGICAL COSTUME TRUNK
and elements from nature.
Each fairy
shall dress in the manner of a
PRINCESS.

Poor, poor Goldie!

Every single other fairy was adorned from head to toe in yards of tulle and silk and lace, and every inch of it was pink. They carried ruby wands and wore diamond tiaras and capes of purest pearl satin. Their shoes were trimmed with feathers, and their hair was piled on top of their heads in beautiful cascading curls. And every fairy's wings were sprinkled with sparkles.

"What's the matter, Golden Bell?" asked Claudine. "Is this how princesses look on Sheep-skerry Island?"

Goldie held absolutely still. She felt as if her witch's dress were sucking all the breath out of her. She wished her broomstick would break into two so she could sink into the floor. She wanted to fly away from this horrible mainland and never come back. But more than anything, she wanted to punch Claudine Townley in the nose.

She did none of these things.

Golden Bell hitched her broomstick under her, straightened her pointy hat, and flew right down into that cloud of pink fairy princesses.

"What are you waiting for?" she said. "Let's go."

sixteen

Off they flew.

It was a long way to Queen Titania's castle.

Goldie's mood, very bleak when she started the flight, lightened as she traveled. She couldn't help herself: She loved flying in the fresh evening air. And she had never traveled on a broomstick! The beating of her wings and the wind in her hair gave her new energy. *I will not be defeated,* she thought as she soared through the night.

The sight of the full moon rising—a bright beacon in the sky—made her think of moonrise on Sheepskerry, and of her sisters waiting for her at home. *What would my sisters do?*

Sensible Clara would take off the green makeup and warts, change into comfy pajamas, and go right to bed, the thought of the party far behind her. *Well, that's out,* thought Golden.

Rosy would forgive Claudine and Amanda, imagining that the Townley sisters must be very unhappy themselves, if they could do such an unkind thing to someone else. Then she would go to the party and applaud when someone else won the prize. *That's really out,* Goldie thought.

Sylva would fly into the fancy-dress party with Squeakie squeaking in her arms, and announce to Queen Titania that there were some very mean fairies on the mainland. Then she'd enjoy herself quite happily, as a witch. *That's not me, either,* thought Goldie.

A lovely length of grapevine caught her eye as she flew. She swooped down to pick it up from the ground where it had fallen.

Goldie heard someone flying nearby. It was Fawn, and she looked absolutely stricken.

Her pretty face was pale as moonlight, and her eyes were huge.

Fawn offered Goldie a bouquet of wild white roses and baby's breath. "I picked these for you in the park."

Goldie took them without a word.

"I'm sorry, Goldie. I didn't know. None of us knew you'd dress like that."

Goldie did not believe that for a second. "You didn't know that Claudine was going to trick me?"

"We didn't! We didn't!" cried Fawn. "I mean, we knew that she would make you choose last—but we only went along with it because you're so inventive! I feel ashamed now, but then I just thought it would give us a little help. I didn't know Claudine told you to be a witch! Nobody knew that!"

"Except maybe Amanda," said Golden.

Fawn nodded her head in dismay. "Yes," she said. "Except maybe Amanda." She looked into Goldie's green face. "What are you going to do, Golden?" she asked. "Are you really going to go to the fancy-dress party like that? I suppose if you tell Queen Titania what the Townley sisters did to you—"

"I will do no such thing," said Goldie, and she scooped up some dark purple leaves from the path below. She had a plan in the back of her mind, though she wasn't quite sure what it was. "Claudine and Amanda played a trick on me. Now I will play a trick on them."

"Oh, don't, Goldie! Please don't make this any worse than it already is."

Goldie just smiled. "Don't worry, Fawn," she said. She plucked a handful of Queen Anne's lace from the roadside. "My trick will be perfectly fair. And it may even teach those fairies a lesson. You wait and see."

seventeen

Golden's keen eye spotted a few more things to pick up as she flew to the castle. If she had not been so excited about her plan, she would have spent a little more time being amazed at the castle when they arrived there. It was unlike anything she'd ever seen— even Queen Mab's palace on Sheepskerry was nothing compared to this! The castle was made of stone, not twigs and leaves, and it was as high as a boulder. Turrets and towers rose from its walls. A drawbridge was let down as the fairies entered. Trumpeter swans paddled in the moat.

And the place was lit from top to bottom with firefly lanterns on the outside and beeswax candles on the inside. What a marvel!

"Shall we wait together till we're called into the ballroom, Goldie?" asked Fawn Deere. She was very loyal under the circumstances. For what fairy princess would want to enter a party with a witch?

"No, Fawn, I'm fine," said Goldie. "I'm just going to make a stop in the fairy powder room and fix my face."

Fawn kissed Goldie on the cheek. "You're very brave, Golden Bell."

"Not so very brave—but I do have some excellent ideas," said Goldie, and she flew off down the long hall to find the fairy powder room. She hoped it would be empty.

It was.

Golden looked at her reflection in the mirror. "I was a fantastic witch," she said to herself. "But now I'm going to be—"

"Oh, Goldie! What are you going to be?" Avery burst through the door. "It's too late to change your costume!"

"Avery! What are you doing here?"

"I told Queen Titania I would work at the

party," said Avery, "because I wanted to be here with you!"

Goldie rushed over and hugged her dear new friend. "I'm so glad you're here, Avery," she said. "You can hold my hand as I make myself into a princess!"

"But how will you do that when you're a witch?" asked Avery.

Golden was pulling the warts off her nose. "Ouch!" she exclaimed. Then she grinned. "Not every princess has to be a pink princess," she said. "I'm going to this fancy-dress party as the Princess of the Night." She scrubbed the green face paint off, and her rosy cheeks shone with excitement. "Just you watch me!"

Then she emptied her pockets. Out fell the vine leaves, the delicate Queen Anne's lace, and some gorgeous dark feathers. She flipped her cape inside out and threaded the ruby leaves through the purple lace. She twisted the baby's

breath around the
vine leaves to make
a crown. She shook
the cobwebs off her
wings. They seemed
to sparkle all on their
own.

"The striped stockings,
Goldie!" cried Avery. "They have
to go!"

Goldie whipped them off. Then she looked at
her scuffed slippers. She tied Fawn's white roses
on them; the evening dew made them shine.

"Is that it?" asked Goldie. "Am I ready to go?"

"You've forgotten to get rid of your witch's
hair!" cried Avery, laughing. "Even a princess of
the night brushes her hair!"

Goldie shook her head and started to untan-
gle the mess she'd made of her long, golden hair.
She combed out the snarls and brushed her hair

till it shone. Then Avery placed the crown on her head.

"Now," said Avery, "you are beautiful. Stay still for one minute and I'll sketch a portrait!" Avery took a pencil and a tiny sketchpad from her pocket and with a few swift lines she drew a lovely likeness of her new friend.

"Oh!" cried Goldie. "It's beautiful!"

Just then the queen's trumpeter swans sounded their fanfare.

"It's time for the costume judging!" said Avery. "Hurry! This is it!"

Goldie gave Avery a quick hug; then the two fairies flew back toward the Great Hall. All the other fairies were gathered behind a curtain, waiting to be called by Queen Titania. One by one they flew into the hall to meet with the queen.

Goldie drew the curtain aside just a little so she could see what was going on. Amanda Townley was breathtakingly beautiful in a knee-length ballerina skirt and a diamond tiara. Claudine was even more elegant in a glorious ball gown with a deep-rose-colored bow. Fawn and the other fairies were gorgeous too, even if it was a little hard to tell them apart.

"I don't mind who wins or loses now," said

Goldie to herself. "I'm just proud to have done my best." She lifted her chin and waited for her name to be called. Her wings were quivering, but even Goldie couldn't tell whether they trembled from excitement or fear.

eighteen

Goldie heard the voice of the queen's lady-in-waiting. "Fawn Deere is the last fairy to compete in the fancy-dress party," she said, checking her list, "as Amanda Townley has informed me that Golden Bell will not be—"

Goldie burst out of her hiding place. "Here I am!" she cried, this time with her eyes wide open. "Golden Crystal Bell, Princess of the Night, flying for Sheepskerry Island and Queen Mab!"

Gone was the hideous witch the fairies were expecting. Before them flew a glorious princess in deepest shades of midnight, with a cape festooned with autumn leaves and a coronet of pure white baby's breath.

Goldie fluttered before Queen Titania's throne. "Golden Bell of Sheepskerry," said the queen in her deep voice. "Is this your idea of a princess?"

"It is, Your Majesty." Goldie rubbed her nose with her sleeve, hoping she'd taken off all the green makeup. "I am a dark princess, and a good princess."

"That is quite an original idea," said Queen Titania. She leaned close to Goldie. "You may not know this, but I was a princess of the night myself. A dark princess. And a good princess. Like you." Then she added in a whisper, "Ask Queen Mab about it. We grew up together, you know."

Goldie beamed.

"Fairies," said Queen Titania, "who will our

costume winner be tonight?"

Avery was the first to cheer. "Goldie!" she cried. "It should be Golden Bell!"

The fairy princesses were quiet for a moment. Then Fawn Deere's applause joined Avery's. Soon all the fairies were cheering. "Hooray! Hooray for Goldie!"

"Stop it!" cried Claudine Townley.

"Stop it at once!" shouted Amanda. But no one paid them any attention.

"Gold-ie!" the fairies cried. "*Gold-ie!* GOLD-IE! GOLD-IE!" All the fairies—with the exception of two—were calling Goldie's name.

Goldie curtsied low before Queen Titania (and she noticed, out of the corner of her eye, that Queen Titania did not have so much as a stitch of pink in her sumptuous gown). The fairies continued their cheers.

"Golden Bell of Sheepskerry," said Queen Titania, "the fairies have declared you the clear

winner. And not even a queen would disagree with them."

Queen Titania's enchanted black cat brought in the prize—a golden medal on a ribbon of purple velvet, which matched Goldie's outfit perfectly.

"I like your mussel shells," said Queen Titania in a whisper. Then she declared, "This is for you, Golden Bell, and for all of Sheepskerry. Take it with my blessing." She turned to the other fairies. "And now, fairy princesses, it is time to celebrate *all* your achievements at our fancy-dress party."

"May the festivities commence!" cried the queen's lady-in-waiting.

The party lasted deep into the night, and Golden was the belle of the ball.

nineteen

Dawn came far too soon the next morning, but Goldie didn't really mind. She had packed up her bags the night before. She was eager to go home. Avery had promised she'd meet her at the dock to say good-bye. How long ago it seemed that she'd first arrived on the mainland! And how much had happened!

Silently she flew down to the big wooden door of the Townleys' fairy town house. Her bags did not seem so heavy now. "Good-bye, Claudine and Amanda," she said. "You gave me a rough ride."

She was just about to slip outside when she saw an envelope on the front table. It was addressed, in very clear writing, to Golden Crystal Bell.

Inside was a letter, which she took her time to read.

Dear Golden,
We're sorry we were so mean to you this weekend. And that ~~we~~ Claudine tricked you into dressing as a witch for the fancy-dress party. We won't do it again. Come back soon (and tell us how you made that leafy cape!).
Your friends, maybe?
Amanda and Claudine

"*Humph*," said Goldie. "I wonder if they mean it." She picked up the letter and tucked it in her shoe bag. "I'll just have to come back to see if they do."

Goldie's sparrow carriage was waiting for her as she left the town house. The chipper little sparrow took her straight down to the dock.

"I guess Avery slept in today, not that I blame her." Goldie sighed. "I will miss her so much when I get back home." The glimmer of an idea shone in the back of her mind, but she didn't quite know what she was thinking. Then she heard the squawk of her sparrow carriage driver.

"We're here already!"

The ferry dock was silent and empty when Goldie arrived. But she was right on time. She could just see Merryweather's nose poking out of the water as the faithful gray seal paddled toward the shore.

Suddenly she heard a rush of wings.

"You made it, Avery!" cried Goldie.

"Of course I did!" said Avery.

"How will we ever get along without each other?" said Goldie. "I wish you could come to Sheepskerry. Then we could see each other every day!"

"Oh, I wish I could!" said Avery.

Merryweather gave three short barks. Suddenly Goldie realized exactly what her idea was.

"But . . . you *could* go with me, Avery," she said. "You could come to the island. You would love it on Sheepskerry. And you wouldn't have to be a serving fairy there."

Avery's face lit up for a second. But then the light dimmed. "How could I leave Caraway Cooke? And my duties in the town house?"

"Caraway's sister could work in the kitchen."

"It's true," said Avery. "She's asked for that a million times."

"Then let her take your place. Oh, you can be a Sheepskerry fairy! And you could live with us. Or . . ."

Suddenly, Golden remembered Faith's voice: *How I would love a little companionship, now that winter is drawing near.*

"Faith Learned will take care of you! Her sisters are all gone."

In an instant, the two fairies had settled everything. While Merryweather played in the bay, Avery sent a homing-pigeon message

to Caraway Cooke. She drew a special message to let Caraway know where she was going and asked her to send along her things. She promised she would write (or draw) a note every week.

"And now," said Goldie, "there's only one thing left to do."

"What's that?" asked Avery.

"To say: Let's be best friends."

"Yes!" cried Avery, and she threw her arms around Goldie. "Let's be best friends."

Merryweather barked again. The tide was turning.

"Time to go!" said Goldie. She jumped aboard. "Coming?"

"Coming," said Avery.

As the sun rose and Merryweather paddled toward the distant shore, Goldie held Avery's hand. "What a lot we will have to tell my sisters!" she said. Then she turned and looked behind her. The towering buildings were getting smaller and smaller. "Good-bye, mainland," she said. "Thanks for my very first—solo!—adventure. I'll be back again. Pretty soon."

fairy secrets

Squeak's Words

Doh-ca!: Me too!

Ma-bo-bo: I love you.

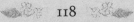

How to Make a Fairy Princess Cape like Goldie's

This is a perfect project for a rainy day.
You'll need a grown-up to help!

W hat you'll need:

• A large piece of cloth from a Magical Costume Trunk. If you do not have a Magical Costume Trunk, then you'll need to buy a piece of fabric from a fabric store, or perhaps you have something at home that you could use.

• A long piece of ribbon to tie your cape, maybe one yard long.

• Fabric glue, or a sewing machine (or a needle and thread, if you're the Stitch sisters).

• Decorations—feathers, felt flowers, ribbons, glitter glue, or anything you like.

How to make the cape:

Cut the piece of fabric so that it makes the kind of cape you'd like to wear. It can be a square or a rectangle, or a semicircle. Whatever you like best.

Place the ribbon along the top of the fabric, about $1/2$" below the fabric's edge.

Squeeze a thick line of fabric glue along the edge of the fabric, below the ribbon.

Fold the edge of the fabric over the ribbon to create a hem, being careful not to touch the ribbon with the glue.

Let the glue dry. (If you sew the hem, there's no drying time!)

Decorate the outside of the cape with the decorations. And if your cape is reversible, decorate the inside, too.

Tie it loosely around your neck, and twirl!

Fairy Bell Sisters' Farewell Song

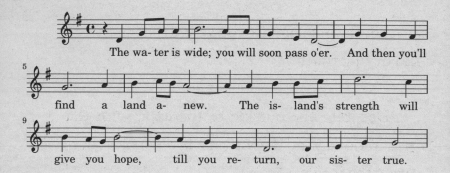

The wa-ter is wide; you will soon pass o'er.   And then you'll

find   a   land a- new.   The is-   land's   strength   will

give you hope,   till you re- turn,   our sis- ter true.

An excerpt from

Clara
and the
Magical Charms

The Fairy Bell Sisters

Book 4

The five Bell sisters—and their friend Poppy Flower—were making their way back from fairy school, which had let out early today, as the snow was falling fast and thick. They darted between snowflakes as they flew.

"Gnomes *are* lots of fun," said Goldie, "even if too many of them wear those awful pointy hats."

"I like their hats!" said Rosy.

"Tutu!" said Squeak.

"Me three!" said Sylva. "And I don't mind what they wear as long as they're not too good at sports. Because I want to beat them all at the Valentine's Games."

That's another thing the fairies love about February: the Valentine's Games. I won't tell you about them now, as Rosy will tell us about them in a moment or two, *if* you can be patient.

"The only way you'd beat *all* the gnomes in your very first year of competition," said Goldie, "is if you used magic, which unfortunately we don't have much of yet."

"Not true!" said Sylva. "I've been training! Besides, I'll have lots of magic soon."

"Not too soon, I hope," said Rosy. "We still have some growing up to do before we get our magical powers." Rosy gave Sylva a hug on the wing. "But I'm sure when you do you'll be as magical as Tink herself."

That made Sylva smile. And though none of her sisters saw it, Rosy's words made Clara smile, too. She wasn't ready to tell her sisters— yet—but she knew her magical powers were growing. She had been practicing her fairy charms since her last birthday, and she could already make a bell ring without touching it. (She was a Bell sister, after all!) Just last week, she'd taught herself how to make a rose bloom in the snow. Right now, she was working on her sparkle charm. That was a tricky one.

As Clara flew toward home, she thought about something that had happened long ago, when she was a very young fairy. She had noticed a tiny grasshopper in the tall grass near Lupine Pond. Its leg was broken, so it could not hop or even sing a grasshopper song to summon help. (Grasshoppers use their legs to make their songs!) Clara had known she didn't have a hope of helping the grasshopper—she hadn't even started learning charms yet at school. But she couldn't bear to see the injured insect. But all at once, she recalled a charm she'd heard her big sister, Tinker Bell, recite once, long ago. How did it go?

Clear as crystal, Clara heard Tink's voice in her head. She closed her eyes, stretched out her arms, and said:

Harm and hurt
And pain no more.
Feel this power,
From my core.

May you be
Sound as a bell.
May my magic
Make you well!

Clara had felt faint and dizzy, and it took a few moments before she was well enough to open her eyes again. She steadied herself and looked at the grasshopper. It hadn't hopped away. It was exactly where she had first seen it. Her charm had failed!

But the very next moment she heard a tiny little *chirrp* coming from her grasshopper friend. That could only mean . . .

"Your leg has healed!" she'd cried.

Then she'd heard a voice behind her. "Clara. Clara Bell."

It was Queen Mab! Clara had nearly jumped out of her wings.

"Were you using magic?"

Clara almost had not dared to speak to the queen. But Queen Mab had asked her a question, and she could not let it go unanswered. "I was, Your Majesty," she'd said.

"The healing charm is very powerful, Clara Bell. Did you learn it from Tinker Bell?"

"I did, Queen Mab."

"Tink should know better than to teach that to you. It takes life to heal life."

Clara wasn't exactly sure what Queen Mab had meant when she said that. But she had curtsied deeply. "Forgive me, my queen," she'd said.

"Do not be ashamed, Clara Bell. You are a young fairy right now, but you have a gift for magic. You will be a very great fairy one day."

Clara could hardly believe her ears. "I will?" she'd asked in a whisper.

"Yes, Clara Bell, you will," said Queen Mab.

Meet the
Fairy Bell Sisters!